TIMELESS CLASSICS

GREAT EXPECTATIONS

Charles Dickens

– ADAPTED BY –

Patricia Hutchison

SADDLEBACK
PUBLISHING

ᒐ TIMELESS CLASSICS

SADDLEBACK
P U B L I S H I N G
www.sdlback.com

ISBN-13: 978-1-62250-718-4
ISBN-10: 1-62250-718-5
eBook: 978-1-61247-969-9

Printed in Guangzhou, China
NOR/1013/CA21301929

18 17 16 15 14   1 2 3 4 5

| CONTENTS |

| 1 |

A Convict on the Marsh

My last name is Pirrip. My first name is Philip. I put both names together. I call myself Pip.

I lived with my sister and her husband. He was a blacksmith. My first clear memory was when I was seven. I visited my parents' graves. I started to cry.

"Stop that noise!" cried a terrible voice. "Or I'll cut your throat!"

I saw a man. He was scary. He had a leg chain. He grabbed me.

"Please don't cut my throat, sir!"

"Tell me your name!" said the man.

"Pip, sir."

"Where do you live?"

I pointed to our village.

"Where are your mother and father?"

I pointed to their graves.

"Who do you live with? That is, if I *let* you live!"

"My sister. She's married to the blacksmith. Joe Gargery."

"Blacksmith, eh?" he said. "Get me a file. And get me food. Or I'll kill you! Bring them here tomorrow morning. Don't tell anyone about me."

I said I'd do it. Then I ran home.

Joe was in the kitchen. He was a nice man. My sister, Mrs. Joe, wasn't so nice. She beat me. And she beat Joe too.

"Mrs. Joe is very angry," Joe warned. "She's coming! Get behind the door."

My sister found me. "Where have you been?" she asked, hitting me.

I was afraid. But I was more afraid of the man I had met. I thought about stealing the file and the food.

Suddenly I heard loud noise. "Are those guns?" I asked Joe.

"A convict ran off last night. The shot is to warn us. One more has escaped."

"Who's firing?" I asked.

"Guards on the prison ships!" cried my sister. "Criminals are put on those ships. Now go to bed!"

I went up to my room. I was afraid.

At dawn, I went downstairs. The floorboards creaked. I was afraid I'd be caught. I stole some brandy. And bread and cheese. I took a pork pie too. I got a file from Joe's toolbox. Then I ran.

Before long, I saw a man. I touched his shoulder. He jumped. He was not the man I had met! But he *was* a convict. I ran.

Then I found the right man. I gave

him the brandy and food. He ate and drank. I felt sorry for him.

"I'm glad you liked the food. Will you save any for the other man?" I asked.

"What other man?" the convict asked.

"Over there. He's dressed like you. He's got a chain on his leg," I said.

He grabbed me. "Show me where he went. I'll get him! Give me the file!"

He filed the chain like a madman. I was afraid again. I left him working at the metal.

| 2 |
The Capture

I thought I'd be arrested for stealing the food. But Mrs. Joe was busy getting ready for Christmas.

"Where have you been?" she asked.

I told her I'd been down at the village to hear Christmas songs. She hadn't noticed anything missing.

Mr. Pumblechook came for dinner. He was a well-off village merchant.

We all sat down to eat. My sister talked about the trouble I'd caused her. Then she stood up. "You must taste my pork pie," she said.

She went to get the pie. I ran for my life. I hurried to the door. There, I ran into some soldiers. They had guns. One had handcuffs. Mrs. Joe came running.

"I need the blacksmith to fix these handcuffs," said a soldier.

"Are you after the convicts?" asked Mr. Pumblechook.

"Two of them! Has anyone seen them?" the soldier asked.

Everyone said no, except me. No one noticed me.

Joe fixed the handcuffs. He got his coat. He said we should all go and help with the hunt.

Joe and I kept to the back. "I hope we don't find them," I whispered.

"I hope they've escaped," Joe said.

I rode on Joe's shoulders. I looked around. Would my convict see me? Would he think I turned him in?

Suddenly, we stopped. There was shouting. The soldiers ran. Joe ran too.

"Here they are!" a soldier shouted. He pointed his gun at the bottom of a ditch. "Give up, you two!"

The convicts were fighting. The soldiers dragged them out of the ditch.

"He tried to murder me!" the other convict said.

"He lies!" my convict shouted.

My convict turned around and saw me. I tried to show I had not turned him in. He gave me a look I didn't understand.

My convict turned to the soldiers. "I

took some food from the blacksmith's. I'm sorry to say, I've eaten your pie."

"We don't know what you've done," Joe said. "But we wouldn't want you to starve to death. Would we, Pip?"

The prisoners were taken back to the ship. I never told anyone about my convict. I was afraid to lose Joe's trust.

———— ••• ————

When I was older, I would work with Joe. I would be a blacksmith too. Until then, I did odd jobs.

The village school met each evening.

Our teacher napped through most classes. She also had a little store. A girl named Biddy helped her. She was an orphan too. I learned the alphabet with Biddy's help.

One night, I wrote Joe a note. He looked at it with pride. "How smart you are! Why don't you teach me to read?"

Mrs. Joe had gone to the market. Joe made a fire. He swept. We waited for her to return.

Mrs. Joe ran into the house. "Now if this boy isn't grateful today, he never will be! Miss Havisham wants him to go and play there. So of *course* he's going. And he'd *better* play there!"

Everybody had heard of old Miss Havisham. She was a grim, old rich lady. She lived in a big house. She never came out.

I was scrubbed and dried. I was put into a stiff suit. Mr. Pumblechook was taking me to his home in town. Then to Miss Havisham's in the morning.

I had never been away from Joe before. "Good-bye, Joe," I said sadly.

"Good-bye, Pip!"

Questions ran through my mind. Why was I going to Miss Havisham's? What was I supposed to play at?

| 3 |

Miss Havisham and Estella

I stood outside Miss Havisham's gate at 10:00 a.m. Her house was old and dark. The windows had rusty bars. I rang the bell.

A young lady came across the courtyard. "So this is Pip?" she asked in a proud voice. "Come in, Pip."

She was beautiful. And about my age. We went up some stairs. At last we came to a door. "Go in," she said. Then she walked away.

I was half afraid. I knocked. A voice said to enter.

The room was lighted with candles. I saw a cloth-draped table. There was a mirror on it. Sitting in an armchair was a lady. The strangest lady I'd ever seen.

She was dressed for a wedding. In lace and silk. She wore a veil. There were flowers in her hair. She wore just one shoe. Half-packed trunks filled the room.

Everything should have been white. But it was all faded and yellow. The bride in the gown was old and wrinkled.

"Who is it?" said the lady.

"It's Pip, ma'am. I'm here to play."

"Come closer. Let me look at you."

I saw her watch had stopped at 8:40. A clock was stopped at the same time.

"Look at me. I have not seen the sun since you were born. Are you afraid of me?" asked Miss Havisham.

"No," I lied.

She put her hand on her chest. "Do you know what I touch here?"

"Your heart?" I asked.

"Yes, and it's broken!" She smiled strangely. "Now, I want to see some play. Call Estella!"

I called. And Estella came.

"Let me see you play cards with this boy," Miss Havisham said to her.

"With *him*? He's nothing but a common working boy!" Estella said.

I thought I heard Miss Havisham whisper, "Well then, you can break his heart."

The old lady watched us play the game.

"His hands are rough," Estella said. "And what ugly boots he wears."

I played the game. Estella won. She threw her cards down.

"Go now, Pip," said Miss Havisham. "Come again in six days. Estella, take him downstairs. Give him something to eat."

I followed Estella down the stairs.

"You wait here," she ordered.

I looked at my hands. And then at my boots. They had never bothered me before. But they did now.

Estella came back with bread and meat. She put it on the ground. She was treating me like a dog. Tears came to my eyes. It made Estella smile. I held them back. I wouldn't let her see me cry.

"Why don't you cry?" Estella asked.

"Because I don't want to," I replied.

"You're almost crying." She laughed. Then she pushed me outside the gate. And she was gone.

I leaned on the wall and cried. I started back home. I thought about being a common working boy.

My sister wanted to know about Miss

Havisham. I thought it was wrong to say how she really was. So I made up stories. I said she sat in a black velvet coach. Estella served her cake on a gold plate.

But I couldn't lie to Joe. I told him about the beautiful young lady who had called me common.

I went to my room. I said my prayers. I thought about my day. I fell asleep.

I changed that day. Stop a moment. Take a day from your life. Think how different your path would be without it.

| 4 |
A Coin and a Kiss

One day I awoke with an idea. I knew how I could make myself less common.

I asked Biddy to help me with school. She agreed. I started studying very hard.

I went to the village bar to pick up Joe. He was with a man I didn't know.

"What do you call him?" he asked Joe.

"Pip," Joe answered.

"Is he your son?"

Joe told him why I lived with him. He said I would work with him one day.

The stranger kept looking at me. He stirred his drink with a file. It was the file I had given to my convict. The stranger knew the convict. He knew me too.

We started to leave. The man stopped us. "Here you go, boy," he said. He handed me a coin wrapped in paper.

I thanked him. I held tight to Joe.

My sister took the coin. It was wrapped in paper money! This made her very happy.

I had bad dreams that night. I saw the file coming at me. I couldn't see who held it. I woke up screaming.

Soon it was time to go back to Miss Havisham's. Estella let me in. She took me to a room. "Stay here, boy," she ordered.

Estella called for me. I followed her down a dark hall. She stopped.

"Well?" she said. "Am I pretty?"

"I think you're very pretty," I said.

Then she slapped my face. "Why don't you cry, you common boy?"

"I will never cry for you again." This was a lie. I was crying inside.

Estella left me with Miss Havisham. I followed her to a dark room. It was thick with dust. There was a long table. On it was an object. An old wedding cake! There were cobwebs on it. I saw crawling spiders. I heard mice too.

"Today is my birthday," she said. Then Estella came in.

"Now let me see you two play!" Miss Havisham said.

We played cards. Estella beat me again. She was rude. I found my own way out.

I met a young man near the gate. "Who let you in?" he asked.

"Miss Estella."

"Come and fight," he said. He hit me in the stomach.

I knocked him down. Bloodied

his nose. He got to his feet. "Good afternoon," he said.

Estella was waiting at the gate. "You may kiss me if you like," she said.

I kissed her cheek. It meant nothing to her.

Estella never asked me to kiss her again. Sometimes she was nice to me. Other times she was cruel.

"Isn't she pretty?" Miss Havisham would often ask. Then she would whisper to Estella, "Break their hearts!"

My sister waited for Miss Havisham to give me money. None was offered.

| 5 |

A Young Man of Great Expectations

One day Miss Havisham looked closely at me. "You're growing tall!" she said. "What's the name of that blacksmith?"

"Joe Gargery, ma'am."

"The time has come. You must be his trainee. Bring him here."

The next day, Joe dressed in his best clothes. We set off for Miss Havisham's.

Estella showed us in. Joe was quiet.

Miss Havisham held out a bag. "Pip has earned this by coming here," she said.

The bag held 25 pounds! She said two things. I would work with Joe. And, I should expect no more favors from her.

"Will I come here again?" I asked.

"No," Miss Havisham said. "Joe is your master now."

My sister was happy with the money. We celebrated. But I didn't enjoy it. I no longer wanted to be a blacksmith.

I didn't tell Joe how I felt. I worked hard for him at the forge. But I was always afraid Estella would see me.

Joe had another helper. He was a mean man named Orlick. I had always been afraid of him.

One morning I asked Joe for a half-day off. I wanted to visit Miss Havisham. Both Joe and I knew I really hoped to see Estella. Joe let me go. Orlick went crazy. Joe gave him time off too.

Miss Havisham knew why I'd come. She told me Estella was away at school. Then she sent me away. I headed home unhappy.

I met Orlick on the road. "Did you hear them?" He told me guns were fired from the prison ships. Convicts had escaped again.

Then Mr. Pumblechook came running. "Convicts broke into your house!" he shouted.

I ran home. My sister had been hit on the head. She was on the floor. Next to her was my convict's chain. But I knew he didn't hit her. Maybe it was Orlick. Or the strange man at the bar. He'd had Joe's file.

My sister lived. She wasn't as mean. She couldn't hear well. And she couldn't speak.

Biddy now lived with us. She helped take care of my sister.

———— ••• ————

Four years passed. A group of us were at a bar. I saw a man watching us.

"Is one of you Joe Gargery?" he asked.

"I am," said Joe.

"Is your trainee here? Where is Pip?"

"Here," I said. I had seen him at Miss Havisham's.

"I'm Mr. Jaggers. I'm a lawyer. I can't tell you my client's name," he said.

"But my client has money for you. You will move to London. You will become a young man of great expectations."

I was sure his client was Miss Havisham.

"You must never know my client's name. So don't ask. And you can't change your name," Mr. Jaggers said.

He gave me money to buy clothes. I now had a tutor, Mr. Pocket. I would meet him next week in London.

Later, Joe told Biddy my news. They said they were happy. But their voices were sad.

The day came. I dressed in my new clothes. I told Joe that I wanted to walk to the coach alone. I told him it would be too hard to say good-bye. But I knew the truth. I didn't want to walk beside Joe in his plain clothes.

I said my good-byes. They hugged me. Biddy wiped her eyes.

I broke down as I walked. I wanted to go back. I wanted to say good-bye again. But I got on the coach. The world lay before me.

———— ●●● ————

This is the end of the first stage of Pip's expectations.

| 6 |

London

London frightened me. The streets were ugly, crooked, and dirty.

I went to Mr. Jaggers' office. I could see he was a busy man. He told me I would stay at an inn. On Monday I would go to meet my teacher, Mr. Pocket.

Jaggers' clerk, Wemmick, showed me to the inn. "We will meet again," he said. The inn was a run-down place. This was the first day of my great expectations. It was not what I thought.

I was met by Mr. Pocket's son, Herbert. He was the boy I had fought with at Miss Havisham's! We both burst out laughing. I politely shook his hand.

"I'm happy for your good luck," said Herbert. "Did you know Miss Havisham sent for me before you came? Estella didn't like me. I didn't like her either. She's stuck up. And Miss Havisham taught her to get revenge on all men."

"Why would Estella get revenge on all men? Revenge for *what*?" I asked.

Herbert Pocket began his tale. "Miss

Havisham's father was rich. He spoiled her. His wife died, and he married again. They had a child. A son. They named him Arthur. He wasn't a good person. Mr. Havisham left his fortune to his daughter. Arthur was angry.

"Arthur found a man to go after Miss Havisham. He won her trust. She gave him her heart. She gave him money. She planned to marry him. My father tried to warn her. The wedding day came. But the groom never did. He wrote a letter—"

I broke in. "Did it arrive as she was dressing for her wedding? Was it 8:40?"

Herbert nodded. "She stopped all the clocks. The wedding never took place.

Miss Havisham kept everything the way it was. She hasn't gone outside since."

"What happened to the groom?" I asked. "Is her brother still alive?"

"That's all I know," Herbert said.

We ate together that evening. I asked Herbert what he did for a living. He said something about insuring ships. I wondered why he lived in such a shabby place. I asked him what ships he insured.

"Well," he said, "I'm looking for the right chance."

He wasn't rich, but he was cheerful. We got along well.

| 7 |

Dinner Parties
and a Visit from Joe

On Monday, I dined with Herbert at his father's house. Mr. Pocket did not make much money as a teacher. To pay the bills, he rented rooms to two students. One's name was Drummle. He was an odd-looking man. I didn't like him from the start. I liked the other young man, named Startop.

My next invitation was from Mr. Jaggers. I was told to bring Herbert,

Startop, and Drummle. Jaggers took an interest in Drummle. He was a loud, sulky fellow.

Dinner was served by a housekeeper. Jaggers called her Molly. She was tall and pale. She had large, faded eyes. I felt I had seen those eyes before.

Jaggers grabbed her hand. "If you want to see strength, look at this." There were deep scars across Molly's wrist.

"There's real power in this hand," said Jaggers. "Few men are as strong.

"It's late. We must break up the party," Jaggers said. He raised his glass. "Drummle, I drink to you."

I spent my days learning how to become a gentleman. I also spent a lot of money. I bought furniture and clothing.

Soon I received a letter from Biddy. Joe was coming to London! I was not happy. I didn't mind if Herbert met him. But I didn't want Drummle to see my common friend.

Joe arrived the next day. His face was glowing. He shook my hand. "My, you've grown!" he said.

I asked about my sister and Biddy. Biddy was teaching Joe to read and write. Our visit went on. Joe became uncomfortable. He began to call me "sir." This made me angry. I didn't know it was all my fault. I sounded different. I didn't act like I used to.

Joe stood up to leave. "I have one message to give you, sir," he said. "It comes from Miss Havisham."

"Miss Havisham?"

"She says Estella is home. She would like to see you."

I felt my face turn red. "Are you leaving, Joe?" I asked. "I hope you will come back for dinner."

"No, I won't," said Joe. "Pip, I feel silly in this suit. I'm not comfortable. Think of me with my hammer in my hand. Then you'll like me again. Bless you, old chap."

He went out. I hurried after him. But he was gone.

The next day I returned to the village. I went straight to Miss Havisham's. I was greeted by a new gatekeeper. It was Orlick! He greeted me with a frown.

I went up the dark stairs. I knocked on Miss Havisham's door. She was wearing the same yellowed dress.

There was an elegant lady sitting next to her. It was Estella! I hardly knew her. She was more beautiful than ever. I felt like a common boy again.

"Do you find her changed, Pip?" asked Miss Havisham. Her look was mean and greedy.

"And, Estella, is he changed?" Miss Havisham asked.

We were sent out to the garden. "You must not love me, Pip," Estella said.

"I have no heart. There is no softness there."

We returned to the house. I went alone to Miss Havisham's room. She whispered, "Love her, love her! I raised her to be loved. I made her what she is. Real love means giving up your whole heart and soul … as I did!"

That night I lay in my bed at the village inn. I should have gone to see Joe. Tears came to my eyes. Then I thought of Estella. She would find Joe common. I stopped crying. God forgive me.

| 8 |
Coming of Age

I returned to London. I had not visited Joe. I sent a gift to ease my guilt. Then I went to see Herbert.

"Herbert, I *adore* Estella," I said.

"Lucky for you. You were picked out for her. How does she feel about it?"

I shook my head and frowned.

"Pip," Herbert said. "Think of the

way Estella was raised. Your future may be miserable."

"I know," I said. "But I can't help it!"

"Well, I'm engaged to a wonderful girl," Herbert said. "Her name is Clara. She lives with her sick father. As soon as I have a job, I will marry her."

Later, I got a letter from Estella. It said that she would be visiting London in two days.

I couldn't eat. I was too excited. Finally it was time to meet her coach. She looked more beautiful than ever.

"I am going to Richmond. You are

taking me there. I'll live with a lady who knows the best people."

I told her Richmond wasn't far. I hoped to visit her a lot.

"Oh, you will see me. It's part of Miss Havisham's plan."

I took her to the house in Richmond. I stood looking at it. I thought how nice it would be to live with Estella. But I had never been happy with her.

I had grown used to spending a lot of money. Herbert spent a lot too. He was soon deep in debt. I offered to give him money. But he was too proud to accept it.

One night a letter dropped through the slot. It said that my sister had died. I had been afraid of her. But I was still sad.

I went to the funeral. Later, I had dinner with Joe and Biddy. I told them I would visit soon. Joe was pleased. Biddy looked doubtful.

The day before my 21st birthday, a note came from Jaggers. He asked me to see him the next day.

"Pip, you are deeply in debt," Jaggers told me. "Here is 500 pounds. This is what you will have to live on each year. You will be handling everything yourself from now on."

I had a great idea. I would use half my money to help Herbert. He could start his own business! I would do it secretly.

Soon after, Herbert came home grinning. He told me that an opening had come up for him at last. I was glad to see him so happy. At last my expectations had done someone some good.

I couldn't stop thinking about Estella. Another shock came to me. Estella had been seeing Drummle.

"Why do you smile at him?" I asked. "You never smile at me that way."

"Do you want me to trick you?"

"Are you trying to trick *him*?" I asked.

"Yes, and many others. But not you. I can't say anymore."

My heart was broken. But then something even worse happened.

| 9 |
The Visitor

I was now 23 years old. I still didn't know who was behind my expectations. Herbert was away on business. I was alone. I heard someone on the stairs.

"Who's there?" I called out.

"I'm looking for Mr. Pip," a voice called.

"That's me." I looked out my door. I saw a man's face. I didn't recognize him.

He pulled off his hat. He tied a handkerchief around his head. I knew him! It was my convict. He moved to hug me. "I have never forgotten what you did for me," he said.

I stopped him. "We can never be friends!" I said.

His eyes filled with tears. "I did not mean to speak harshly," I said. "I wish you a good life."

"I have been living well. I breed sheep. I live far across the sea." He looked around. "How have you done so well?"

I told him I had been chosen to receive some property.

"*Whose* property?" he asked.

"I don't know," I said.

"Let me guess. You are living on 500 pounds a year. You have a guardian. His name begins with a *J*," my convict said.

The room began to spin. I was sad and ashamed. I gasped for breath. He helped me to the sofa.

"Yes, Pip. I made a gentleman of you. I swore if I ever got rich, *you* would get rich too. I worked hard so you wouldn't have to. I'm your second father! Did you ever think it might be me?"

"Never!" I answered.

I wished he had left me at the forge.

The convict told me he made his fortune in Australia. He had been a prisoner there. "But if I am found in England, I will be hanged," he told me. "Where will you put me?"

I told him he could have Herbert's room. I shuddered. This horrible man had made me rich. Now his life was in my hands.

He went to his room. My life was ruined. Miss Havisham had not helped me. Estella was not meant for me. Then the greatest pain came. I turned my back on Joe because of this convict.

Every noise made me afraid. I thought someone was coming for us. I finally fell asleep. I awoke at five. The wind raged in the darkness.

————— ●●● —————

This is the end of the second stage of Pip's expectations.

| 10 |

The Past Links My Convict to Miss Havisham

"I've decided to tell people you are my uncle," I said the next morning.

"Call me Uncle Provis. My real name is Abel Magwitch," he said. "Provis is the name I used on the ship."

"Were you tried in London?" I asked.

"Yes. Mr. Jaggers was my lawyer."

I then met with Jaggers. I had to know the truth.

"I've been visited by Abel Magwitch. He told me he's my helper."

"It's true," said Mr. Jaggers.

"I'd always thought it was Miss Havisham," I said. "It looked like it."

"Take nothing on looks, Mr. Pip. That's a good rule."

I had to get Magwitch out of England.

The next night, Herbert returned. Magwitch made him swear to keep quiet. Then he began his story.

"I never knew my parents. I was in jail a lot. Years ago, I met a man named Compeyson. That's who I was fighting in the ditch.

"Compeyson had a friend named Arthur. They tricked a rich lady. They made a lot of money. Then Arthur got sick and had a vision. He called out, 'She's here with me. I can't get rid of her. She's dressed all in white. She's coming for me.' Then he died.

"I became Compeyson's new partner. We planned all sorts of crimes. In the end, we got caught with stolen money. We went to court. Compeyson got seven years. His lawyer blamed it all on me. I got 14.

"We were put on the same prison ship. I found out he had escaped too. I hunted him down. I smashed his face."

"Is he dead?" I asked.

"I don't know. I never saw him again."

Herbert pushed a note to me. When Magwitch wasn't looking, I read it.

Arthur was Miss Havisham's brother. Compeyson is the man who was going to marry her.

Magwitch went to bed. "What am I going to do?" I asked Herbert. "I can't accept his money. I'm in debt. I don't have a job. I have *no* expectations!"

"You can work with me!" Herbert said. He still didn't know I'd set up his business.

We had to get Magwitch out of England. I'd go with him. But I wanted to see Estella and Miss Havisham first.

I found them together. "I know who my helper is," I told Miss Havisham. "I always thought it was you."

"Why would I be so kind?" she cried. "Foolish boy!"

I told her she had been unkind to Herbert and his father. I told her I had set Herbert up in business. I explained I couldn't help him anymore.

I turned to Estella. "You know I have always loved you."

"I tried to warn you," Estella said. "I'm going to marry Bentley Drummle."

"*Estella!* I'm begging. Please marry someone better than Drummle."

"I am going to marry him," she said. "You'll forget about me."

"Never! You're a part of me!" I kissed her hand.

Later, Miss Havisham sent me a note. She wanted to see me again.

"I'm not made of stone," she said. "I'll give Herbert some money."

"Thank you, Miss Havisham."

Miss Havisham got on her knees. "Oh, what have I done? I taught Estella to be a cold woman. Please forgive me!"

"I would have loved her anyway," I said gently.

"Forgive me," Miss Havisham cried.

There was nothing more to say. I left. But something felt wrong. I rushed back. Miss Havisham was by the fire. A flame caught her dress. She was on fire! I put it out with my coat.

A doctor was called. He said she must rest in bed. I went in to see her. Again, she said, "What have I done?" I kissed her. All was forgiven.

Back at the inn, there was a note from Wemmick. It read, *Don't go home.*

| 11 |
The Escape

I returned to London. I went to Wemmick's house. He told me my place was being watched.

But he had a plan. "Herbert's friend Clara lives near the river. Somebody could slip on board a boat. And he could stay there, ready to leave."

Magwitch was soon at Clara's house. Herbert and I planned to row him to some foreign ship. I would go along.

One night, I had dinner with Mr. Jaggers. He told me Miss Havisham gave Herbert money. This was the only good thing that had happened.

Molly served our meal. I noticed her eyes. They were Estella's eyes. She was Estella's mother!

I told Wemmick. He said Molly had been put on trial. They thought she'd murdered her daughter. But nobody could prove it.

Magwitch had told Herbert more about his life. He'd had a jealous wife. She was once tried for murder. Mr. Jaggers got her off. Magwitch and his wife had a daughter. His wife killed their child! "It happened three years before you met him in the churchyard. He said you reminded him of his little girl," Herbert told me.

"Magwitch is Estella's father!" I cried. We set the plans for his escape.

But before we got started, I found a letter. It said:

Come to the marshes tonight at nine. I have information about your "Uncle Provis." Tell no one. Come alone.

I went straight to the marshes. "Now I've got you!" a voice growled. Feeling sick, I saw my attacker. It was Orlick!

"Why are you doing this?" I asked.

"Because you're my enemy. You have always been in my way. Now I'm going to kill you, like I killed your sister! I know you're smuggling Magwitch away. Someone wants him."

He raised a stone hammer. I shouted. Someone shouted back. I saw two figures. Orlick began to fight with two men. Then he ran into the darkness.

The next thing I knew, Herbert and Startop were standing over me.

Herbert said he had found my letter from Orlick. He had come after me. Now we had to get Magwitch away!

We chose a cold March day. I didn't know where we were going. I didn't know when I might be back. I just wanted Magwitch safe. We all rowed out. We found a steamship. We said good-bye to Herbert and Startop.

Another boat came alongside. "You have a convict," one of the men shouted. "We are here to arrest Abel Magwitch."

Magwitch was pulled onto the other boat. A man in a hood grabbed him. Magwitch pulled down the hood. It was Compeyson! Suddenly the steamship was right next to us. I heard someone yell. I felt our boat sink.

Herbert pulled me onto the other boat.

Startop was also there. But the convicts were gone. Then we saw a dark object in the water. It was Magwitch! An officer pulled him in. He was chained up.

The steamship drifted away. We gave up looking for the other convict.

Magwitch told me he was hurt. He had struggled with Compeyson. Then Compeyson disappeared.

Magwitch was too ill for prison. He went to a hospital. I was with him often. I owed him that. I did not dislike him now. He was grateful. He had only wanted to help me. He treated me better than I'd treated Joe.

| 12 |
Final Partings and New Beginnings

Magwitch had a hard time breathing. I told him I was sorry he had come back to England for me.

"It's all right," he said. "I have seen my boy. He can be a gentleman without me."

I knew his hopes would not come true. He was a criminal. The state would take everything he owned.

Magwitch became weaker each day. On one visit, I thought he had changed. He looked like he was at peace.

"I know you had a child once," I told him. "I want you to know that she lived. She's a lady now. She is very beautiful. And I love her."

Magwitch held my hand. Then he died.

I prayed, "Be kind to him, Lord. He was a sinner!"

Magwitch was gone. I was alone and in debt. I was very ill. I had no purpose.

One morning, two men were standing

by my bed. "We are arresting you, sir. You will go to debtor's prison."

I could not get up. "I cannot go with you," I said. "I will die."

They left me. I don't know what happened over the next few days. One night I woke up. Joe was beside me.

"Oh, Joe, you break my heart!" I cried. "Please be angry with me. Tell me I was ungrateful. Don't be kind to me!"

"We have always been friends," Joe said. I held his hand. We were happy.

Joe took care of me. He told me all that had happened. Biddy taught him to

read. He married her! Miss Havisham died. She left most of her fortune to Estella. Orlick was caught robbing Pumblechook's office. He was in jail.

I grew stronger. Joe became less easy with me. He began calling me "sir" again. One day I found a note. It read:

You are well again, Pip. You will do better without me.

—Joe

P.S. We will always be friends.

There was a receipt with the letter. Joe had paid my debts.

I followed Joe to the forge. I thanked him and Biddy. I had to leave the country. It was too much. Estella and Drummle married. I couldn't bear it. So I sold what I had. I joined Herbert. I became a clerk. Then I became a partner. I was fairly happy. I wrote often to Biddy and Joe.

Herbert finally learned that I'd helped with his business. He was moved.

I visited Joe and Biddy 11 years later. I met their son. They named him Pip. "We both hoped he'd grow up to be like you," Joe told me.

Joe told me that Estella's husband had treated her badly. Later, he had died in an accident.

I went to Miss Havisham's. The house was gone. I stood in the weedy garden. Someone came toward me.

"Estella!" I cried out.

"I have changed," she said. "The years have been hard. But suffering has given me a heart! Now I know how you used to feel. Tell me we are friends."

"We are friends," I said.

"We will continue to be friends," said Estella.

I took her hand. We walked. I knew we would never part.